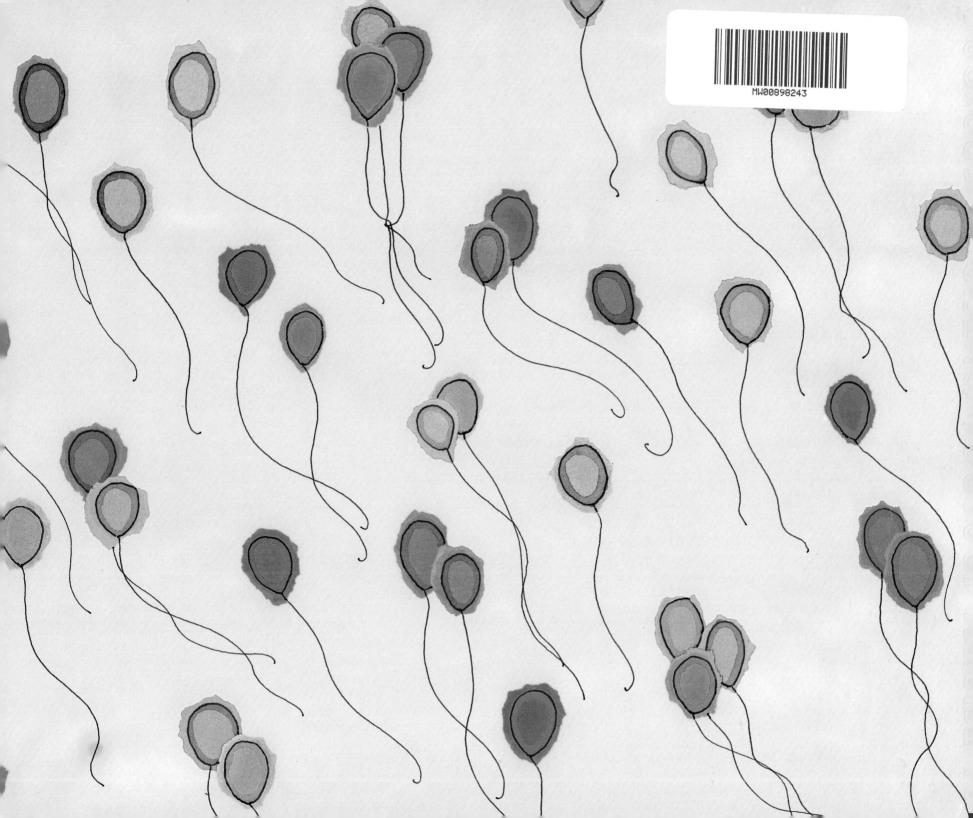

My GraPes

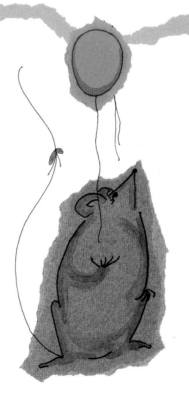

Meggan McGrath

Pfeifer-Hamilton
Duluth, Minnesota

Pfeifer-Hamilton
210 West Michigan
Duluth MN 55802-1908
218-727-0500

My Grapes

Printed in the Republic of Korea by Dong-A Publishing and Printing Company, Ltd.
10   9   8   7   6   5   4   3   2   1

Editorial Director: Susan Gustafson
Art Director: Joy Morgan Dey

Library of Congress Cataloging-in-Publication Data

McGrath, Meggan.
    My grapes / Meggan McGrath.
       p.   cm.
    Summary: A mouse learns to share her grapes with others.
    ISBN 0-938586-99-8 (hardcover) : $16.95
    [1. Mice—Fiction.   2. Grapes—Fiction.   3. Stories without words.]   I. Title.
PZ7.M478528My   1994
[E]—dc20   93-24057
                           AC

Inspired by and dedicated to Anya

I am Morgan Mouse and these are my grapes.

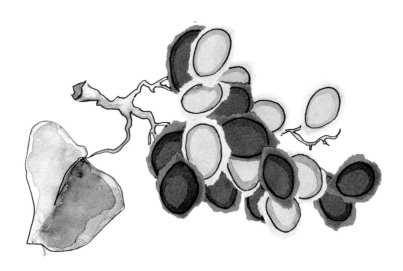

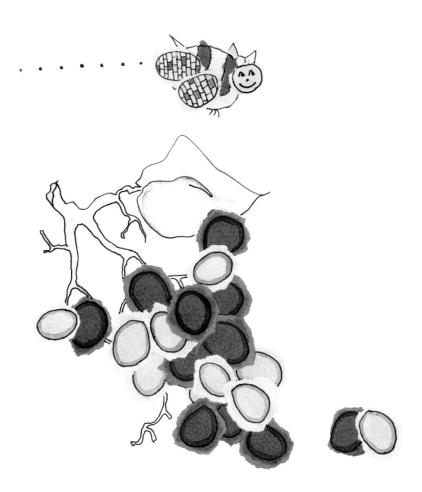

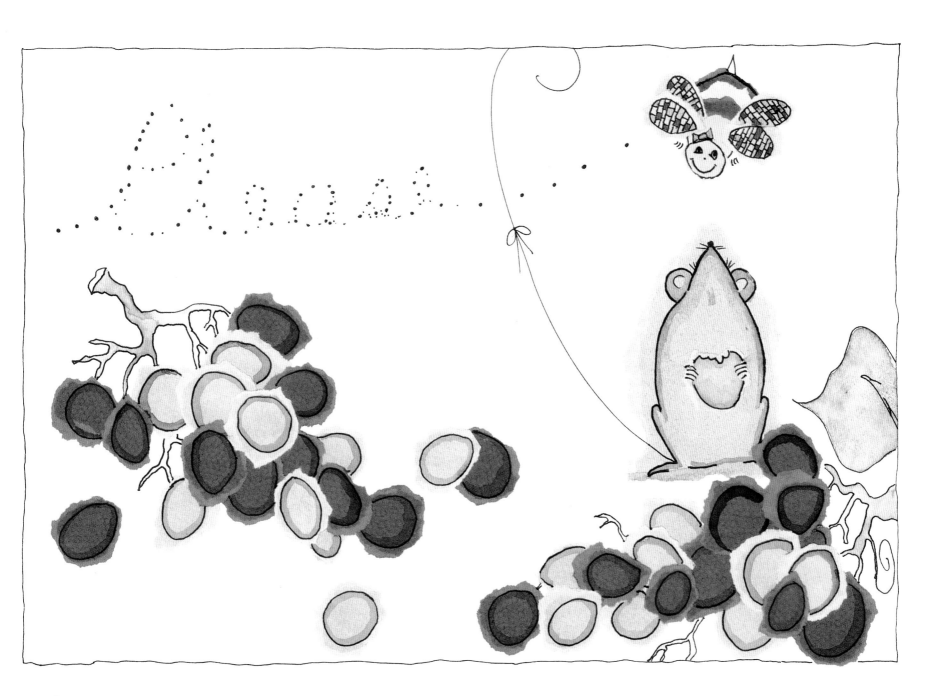

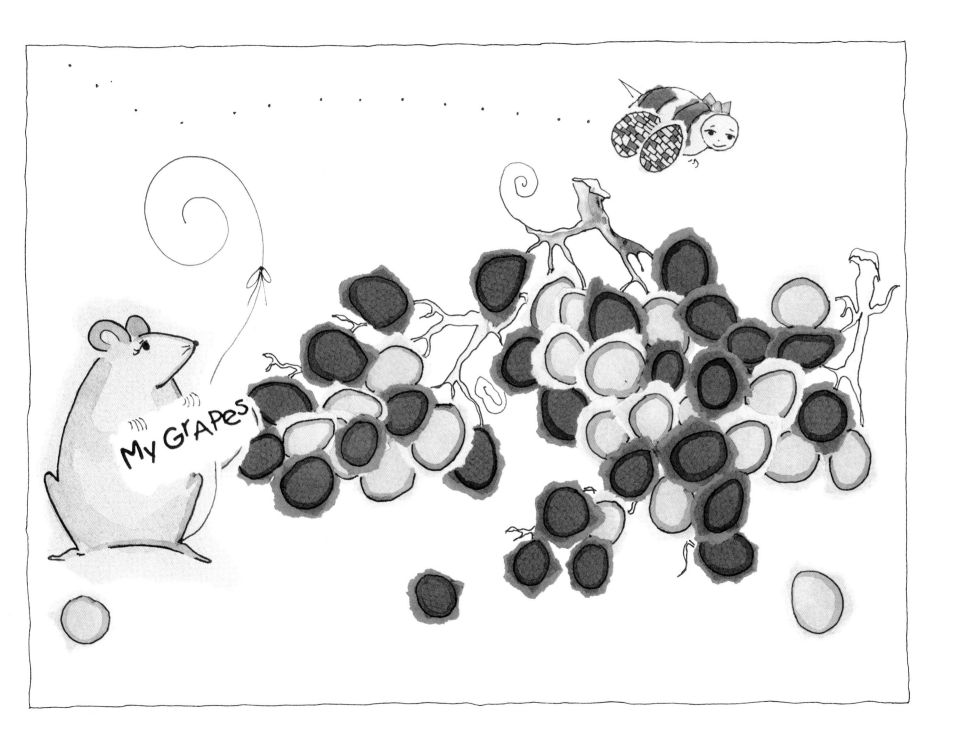

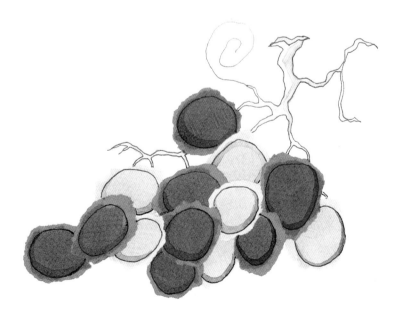

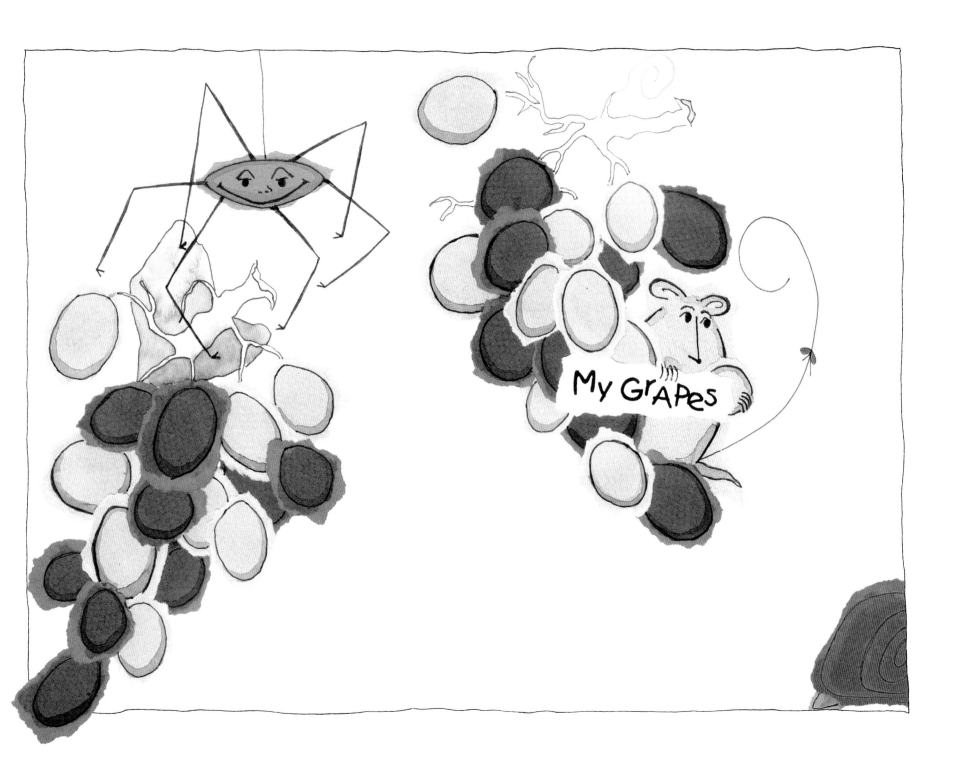

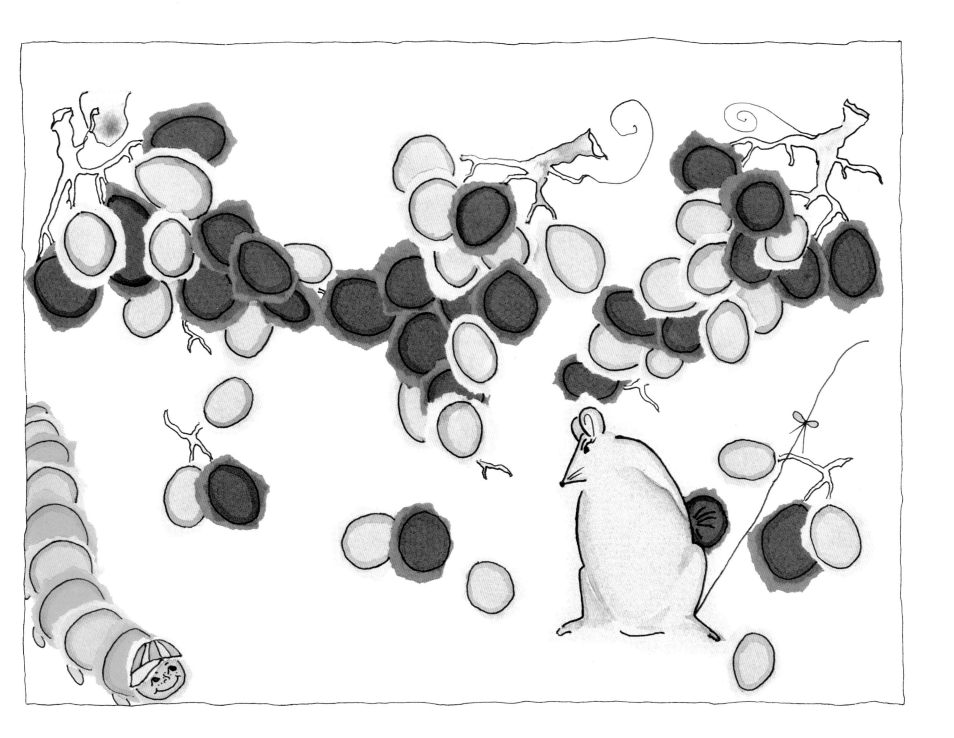

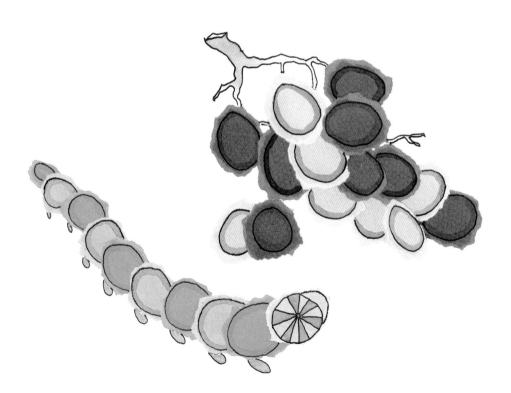

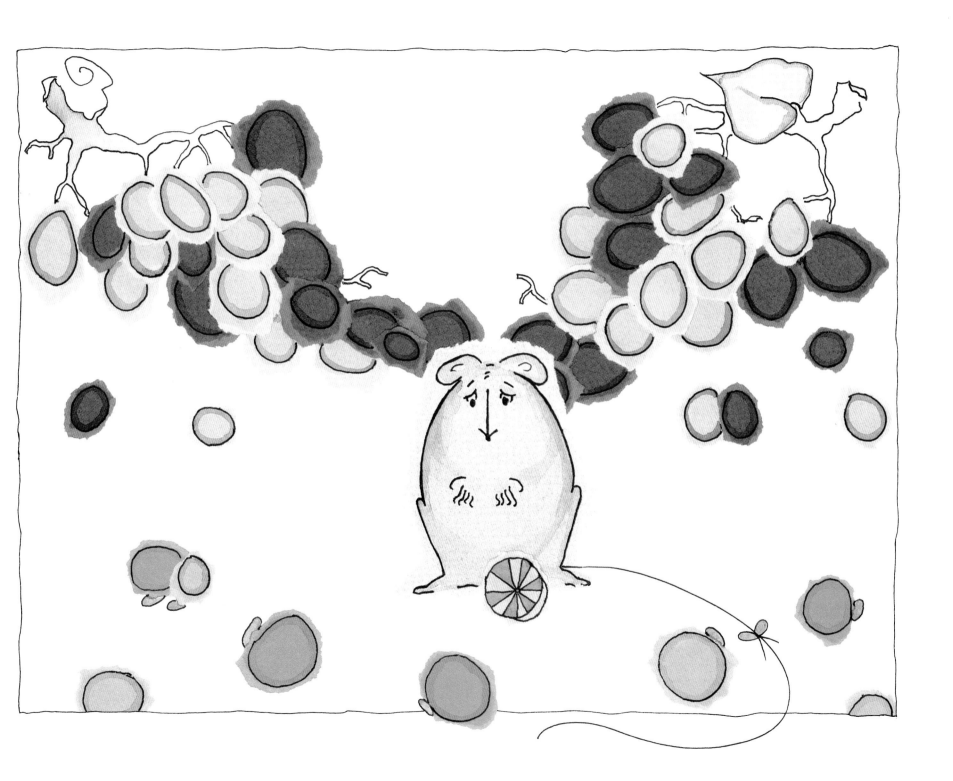

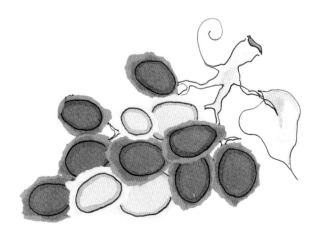

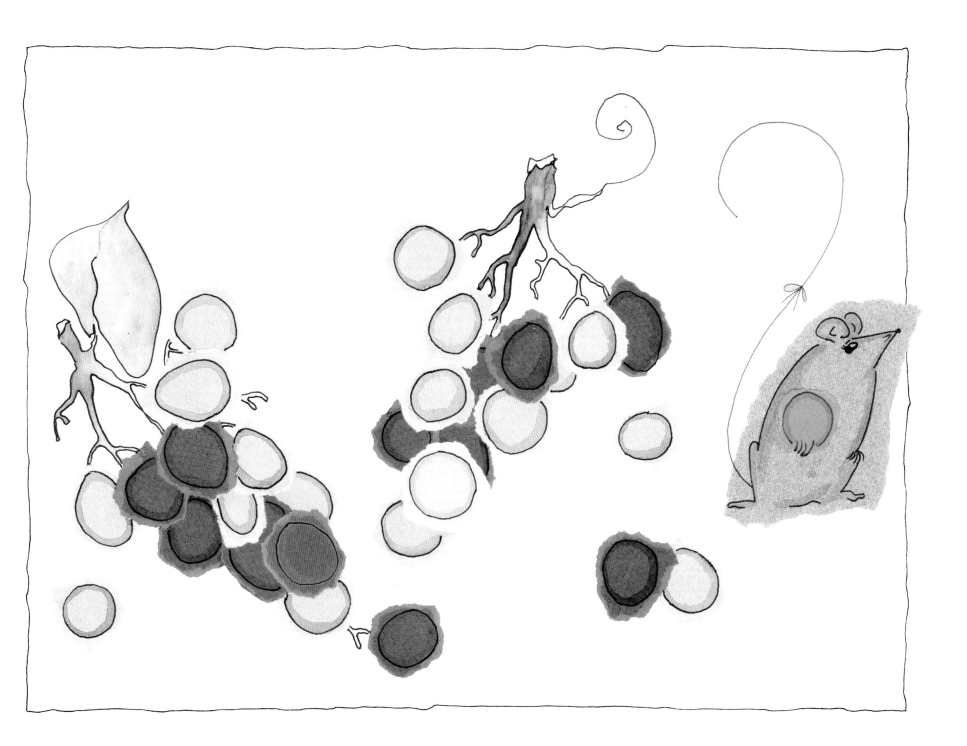

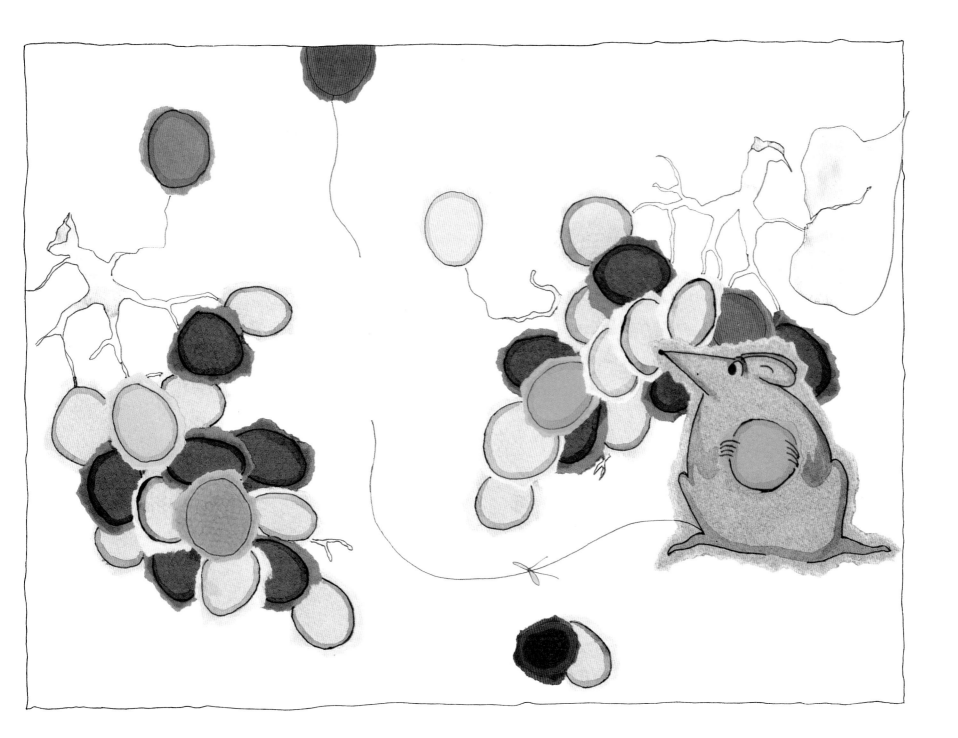

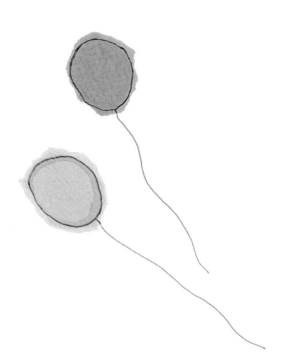

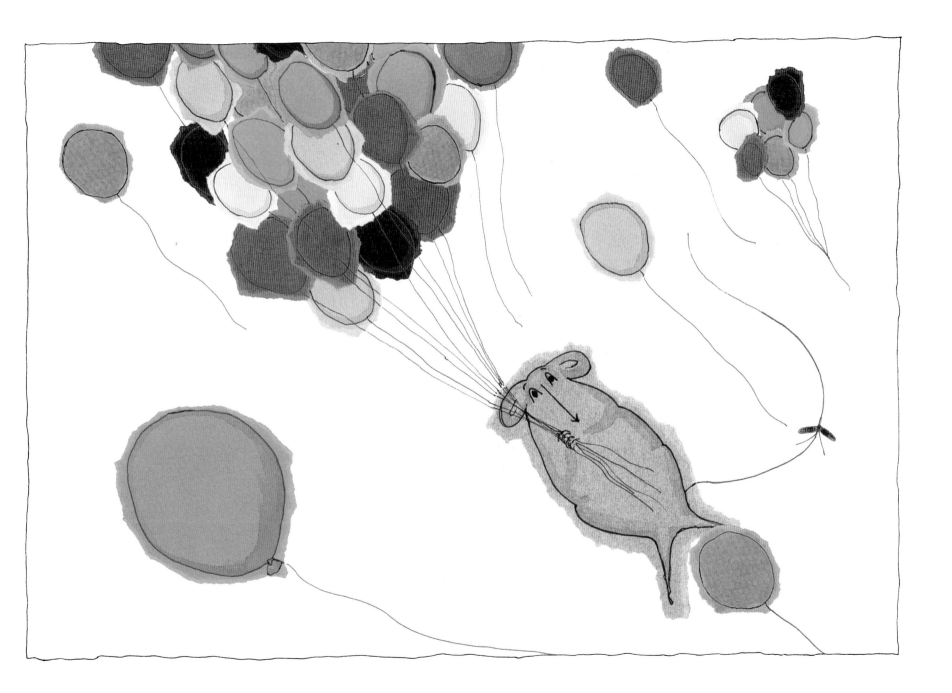

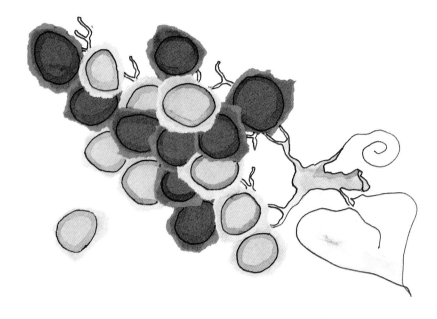

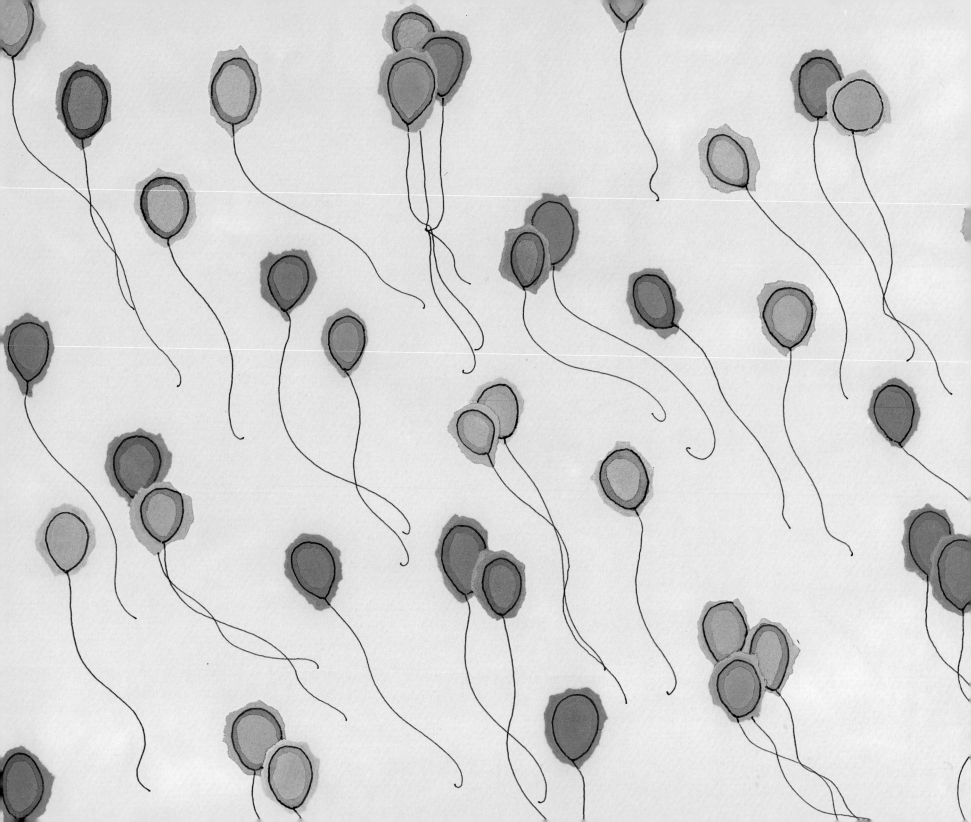